Ladybird Readers

The Big Ship

Series Editor: Sorrel Pitts
Story by Catherine Baker
Illustrated by Chris Jevons

Ladybird Readers Starter Level

Title		Phonics	Sight Words
1	Alphabet Book	A—Z	
2	Is it Nat?	s a t p i n	a is it
3	Nat Sits		an in sit
4	Top Dog and Pompom	m d g o c k	and can I into no
5	Top Dog is Sick		got not
6	The Fun Run	e u r h b f l	at get go has off the to up
7	Gus is Hot!		full his of on put
8	Jazz the Vet	j v w x y z qu	be but had he him she tell was
9	Vick the Vet		did well will
10	Dash and Thud	ch sh th ng	if ran then they with yes
11	Big Bad Bash		big long that this
12	The Big Fish	ai ee oa oo	her look see them
13	The Big Ship		let me my too
14	Martin and Lorna	ar or ur ow oi er	all are for
15	Farmer Carl		cut down good help now
16	The Big Dipper	igh ear air ure	as have like said some went you
17	The Silver Ring		come from so stop we what

First, go through the phonemes on page 4, and do the activity on page 5. Then, read the words in the first half of the book, focusing on pronunciation and blending.

The sight words are introduced in the second half of the book, first on their own and then in full sentences.

At the back of the book, there are activities and assessments practicing phonemes and sight words. These icons indicate the key skills required in each activity:

 Spelling and writing   Speaking   Reading

The Big Ship

Look at the story

First, look at the words and pictures.
Use the words to practice phonics.

Phonics focus

ai   ee   oa   oo

see   look   wait

ship   cool   sail

boat   shoal   loads of rings

Aa Bb Cc Dd Ee Ff Gg Hh Ii Jj Kk Ll Mn

Activity

1 Look. Say the words. Circle and write the correct letters. 🗨✏

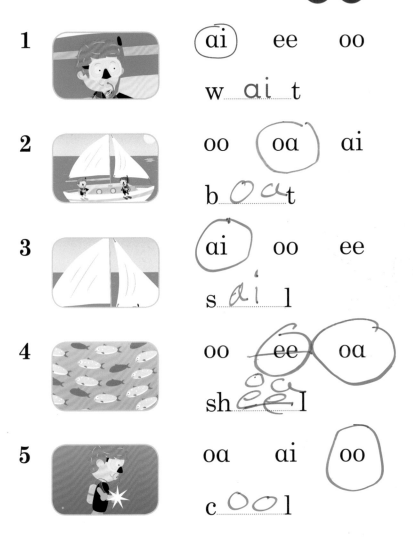

1   (ai)   ee   oo

w _ai_ t

2   oo   (oa)   ai

b _oa_ t

3   (ai)   oo   ee

s _ai_ l

4   oo   ~~ee~~   (oa)

sh _ee_ l

5   oa   ai   (oo)

c _oo_ l

sail

boat

wait

see

shoal

8

cool

see

ship

10

wait

look

loads of rings

look

The Big Ship

Read the story

Now, read the story in full sentences.
Practice using the sight words.

Sight words

let

me

my

too

Jen and Jack sail off
on the boat.

19

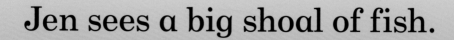

Jen sees a big shoal of fish.

My shot will be cool.

Then, they see a big ship.

Lots of fish will be in this ship.

They see no fish in the ship, but they see a big box!

25

The box has loads of rings and things in it.

Starter

Ladybird Readers — Starter 1 **Alphabet Book**	Ladybird Readers — Starter 2 **Is it Nat?**	Ladybird Readers — Starter 3 **Nat Sits**	Ladybird Readers — Starter 4 **Top Dog and Pompom**	Ladybird Readers — Starter 5 **Top Dog is Sick**
978-0-241-39367-3	978-0-241-39368-0	978-0-241-39369-7	978-0-241-39370-3	978-0-241-39371-0
Ladybird Readers — Starter 6 **The Fun Run**	Ladybird Readers — Starter 7 **Gus is Hot!**	Ladybird Readers — Starter 8 **Jazz the Vet**	Ladybird Readers — Starter 9 **Vick the Vet**	Ladybird Readers — Starter 10 **Dash and Thud**
978-0-241-39372-7	978-0-241-39373-4	978-0-241-39374-1	978-0-241-39375-8	978-0-241-39376-5
Ladybird Readers — Starter 11 **Big Bad Bash**	Ladybird Readers — Starter 12 **The Big Fish**	Ladybird Readers — Starter 13 **The Big Ship**	Ladybird Readers — Starter 14 **Martin and Lorna**	Ladybird Readers — Starter 15 **Farmer Carl**
978-0-241-39377-2	978-0-241-39379-6	978-0-241-39380-2 ✓	978-0-241-39381-9	978-0-241-39382-6
Ladybird Readers — Starter 16 **The Big Dipper**	Ladybird Readers — Starter 17 **The Silver Ring**			
978-0-241-39383-3	978-0-241-39384-0			

LADYBIRD BOOKS

UK | USA | Canada | Ireland | Australia
India | New Zealand | South Africa

Ladybird Books is part of the Penguin Random House group of companies
whose addresses can be found at global.penguinrandomhouse.com.
www.penguin.co.uk   www.puffin.co.uk   www.ladybird.co.uk

**Penguin
Random House
UK**

First published 2017. This edition published 2019
001

Copyright © Ladybird Books Ltd, 2017

Printed in China

A CIP catalogue record for this book is available from the British Library

ISBN: 978-0-241-39380-2

All correspondence to:
Ladybird Books
Penguin Random House Children's
80 Strand, London WC2R 0RL

5 Write the sight words.

my   me   let   too

1   e   m   m   e

2   e   t   l   l   e   t

3   oo   t   t   oo

4   y   m   m   y

31

Assessment

4 Say the words. Put a ✓ by the words with the sound *oa*. 🔘 📖

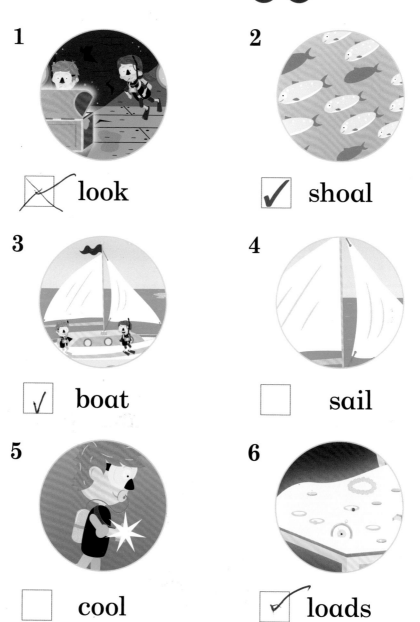

1 ✗ look

2 ✓ shoal

3 ✓ boat

4 ☐ sail

5 ☐ cool

6 ✓ loads

30

3 Read the sight words. Color in the boxes. 📖

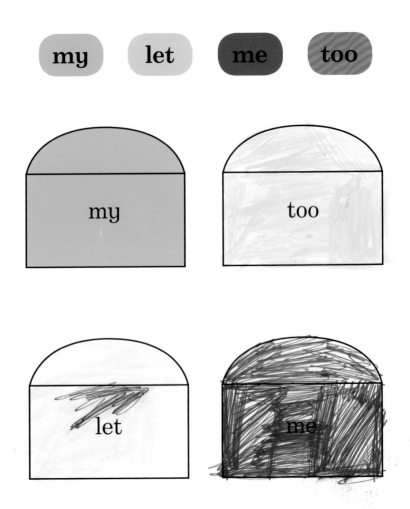

my   let   me   too

Activities

2 **Say the words. Draw the pictures.**
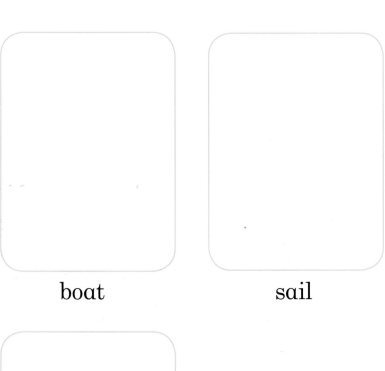

boat

sail

shoal

27